1628

ROOSTERS

SHEILA LAVELLE

Copycat

illustrated by
Stephanie Harris

HODDER AND STOUGHTON
London   Sydney   Auckland   Toronto

British Library Cataloguing in Publication Data

Lavelle, Sheila
  Copycat.
  I. Title   II. Harris, Stephanie   III. Series
  823'.914[J]
  ISBN 0-340-49577-4

First published 1989

Published by Hodder and Stoughton Children's Books,
a division of Hodder and Stoughton Ltd,
Mill Road, Dunton Green, Sevenoaks, Kent TN13 2YJ

Photoset by En to En, Tunbridge Wells, Kent

Printed in Great Britain by T. J. Press (Padstow) Ltd,
Padstow, Cornwall

1 A Spy in the Classroom

It wasn't the spiky ginger hair that made
Mandy stare at the new girl sitting in the
next desk. Mandy had seen plenty of
people with spiky ginger hair, and there
was nothing funny about them at all.

What Mandy hadn't seen before was
somebody with spiky ginger hair poking
out of their earholes. No wonder she
couldn't help staring.

The new girl had appeared in class only that morning. Amber Sunbeam, her name was, and Miss Tubb had cooed with delight at the sound of it.

Mandy and the rest of the class had raised their eyebrows and nudged one another. What sort of a name was that? Amber Sunbeam, my foot, thought Mandy, gazing at the girl's hairy ears and feeling quite unable to tear her eyes away and get on with her work.

It wasn't really noticeable unless you were sitting right next to her, and Miss Tubb, with her thick, heavy spectacles, hadn't noticed at all. Mandy glanced round the room, but everybody was busy working away, and nobody else seemed to have noticed anything strange either.

Just then the new girl glanced up.
She gave Mandy a friendly grin, showing
the sharpest little pointed teeth that
Mandy had ever seen. Then she calmly
got on with what she was doing.

Mandy forced herself to look at her history book, but it was the story of that stupid King Alfred burning the cakes and she was sick of it. Why did you have to have King Alfred's rotten burnt cakes in every class in the school? Did the poor man do nothing else that was worth writing a story about? Mandy sighed and bent her head to her work.

Suddenly a hard finger poked her in the back. It was Louise, Mandy's best friend, who sat in the desk behind.

'Look at that Amber Sunbeam!' hissed Louise. 'Look what she's doing. She's copying the bloomin' history book!'

Copying the history book was Miss Tubb's favourite punishment for all those who dared to be naughty in class. Mandy couldn't imagine anybody wanting to do it for fun. She turned her head to look.

Amber Sunbeam had taken out a tiny black camera, like the ones Mandy had seen in James Bond spy films on the telly. She was rapidly turning the pages of the book, and taking a photograph of each page. When she had finished the history book, she took a school atlas from her desk and started on that, too.

Mandy turned round and gazed at Louise. They stared at one another, breathing heavily.

'And have you seen the length of her fingernails,' whispered Louise in disgust. 'They're like claws!'

'I think she's a spy!' mouthed Mandy, eyes round as pudding plates. And Louise nodded, wriggling with delight.

The bell rang for the end of afternoon
school. The books were put away with
sighs of relief. Thirty pairs of eyes fixed
themselves on Miss Tubb's round
moon-face.

'Class dismissed!' she said at last,
and there was a scramble for the door.

Mandy and Louise were first in the
cloakroom. 'Come on, Lou,' said Mandy,
as they grabbed their coats. 'There's
something dead funny about this Amber
Sunbeam. We're going to follow her
home!'

They waited behind the bike-shed until
the new girl came out. They watched her
walk away from the village in the direction
of Foxes Wood. Then, hearts beating fast,
and clutching at one another, half in fear
and half in excitement, the two friends set
off after her.

2 The Flying Saucer

'Blimey, she doesn't hang about, does she,' puffed Louise as they hurried along, trying to keep the strange girl in sight without being seen themselves.

'Shut up, Lou,' warned Mandy, stepping over twigs that might give out a tell-tale snap. 'She'll hear you.'

They were getting close to a clearing in the deepest part of the wood and the afternoon sun shone down through the leaves, making patterns on the ground. Mandy suddenly put a hand on her friend's arm to warn her, and they dived behind a tree just in time.

The girl in front of them had stopped, and was looking carefully round to make sure she hadn't been followed. Then, satisfied that she was alone, she walked forward into the clearing.

Mandy peered out from behind the tree. In the middle of the clearing, gleaming in the sun, was a small silver spaceship.

'B . . . blimey!' stammered Louise,
digging her fingers painfully into Mandy's
shoulder. 'What's that when it's at home?'

'Sh!' hissed Mandy, her eyes fixed on
the shining silver craft. 'It's a flying saucer.
Our friend here must be from outer
space!'

'Y . . . you mean an ale . . . ale . . .
alien?' gulped Louise, turning as pale as
paper. 'What's she doing here, for Pete's
sake?'

The strange girl had opened the door of the ship, and was carrying something out on to the grass. It looked like a cage of some sort. Then Mandy noticed something else. All around the clearing were similar wire cages, and in each one a bird, or a rabbit, or some other small creature, was hopping or fluttering in an effort to escape.

Mandy watched as the girl put the cage down on the grass, scattered a handful of crumbs inside, and fixed a spring on the door so that it would trap whatever hopped in.

'She's catching birds and things,' Mandy said to Louise in horror. 'What on earth for?'

Then something happened that made the two friends gasp even more. Amber Sunbeam began to peel off her clothes, right there in broad daylight in the middle of the woods.

Off came the sweater, the pink blouse and the striped blue skirt. Off came the canvas shoes and the white cotton tights. Finally, with a huge sigh of relief from Amber Sunbeam, off came the cotton vest and knickers. Mandy goggled, speechless.

'Blimey, it's a bloomin' cat!' said Louise faintly.

It was true. Stripped of her clothes, Amber Sunbeam was covered all over from neck to toe in glossy ginger fur. As the friends watched, stupefied, she dropped down on all fours and gave herself a long stretch, shaking out the kinks in her sleek, white-tipped tail which had been tucked up in her knickers all day. Then she sharpened her claws on a tree-trunk and bent to examine the contents of the cages.

'Flippin' heck!' squealed Louise
fearfully. 'Cats eat birds, don't they. I'm not
staying here to watch this!'
Without making any attempt to move
quietly, she turned and blundered wildly
away through the trees.

Mandy stood still, frozen to the spot.
The strange girl in the clearing had turned
her head at the sudden noise and seemed
to be looking straight at Mandy. Then she
sniffed, mouth slightly open as if tasting
the air, staring with round amber eyes.
Any minute now she'll miaow, thought
Mandy, in a panic.

But when the creature spoke, it was in a
perfectly ordinary voice. 'You can come
out now, Mandy Jackson,' she said. 'I could
do with some help.'

Somehow, forcing one wobbly foot in
front of the other, Mandy walked into the
clearing.

3 **The Copying Machine**

'There's nothing to be scared about,' said the cat-girl, with an angry flick of her tail. 'I'll have to tell you everything now, I suppose. But you must promise not to tell a soul. Cross your heart and hope to die?'

Mandy quickly crossed her heart and hoped to die. The cat-girl led Mandy to a fallen log and pushed her down.

'Sit there,' she ordered. 'I'll show you what I'm doing, and why.'

She disappeared into the spaceship and came out with a sort of cupboard, like a plastic wardrobe with two doors. Then she brought out a cable which she plugged into the back.

The cupboard began to give off a green glow, and Mandy could hear a humming noise. Amber Sunbeam went to one of the cages, grabbed a wriggling rabbit and put it into the left-hand side of the cupboard, pressing a button in a panel on the side.

There was a buzzing noise, then silence. Amber opened the door and lifted out the rabbit, quite unharmed. Putting it on the ground, she gave it a little push.
The rabbit bolted from the clearing so fast Mandy hardly saw it move.

The cat-girl opened the cupboard's
other door. Mandy's eyes widened as she
saw that another rabbit, exactly like the
first one, lay inside. Amber laid it in
Mandy's lap. It was warm and breathing,
but its eyes were closed.

'Is . . . is it all right?' stammered Mandy.

'Of course it is, silly,' said Amber.
'It's just in a very deep sleep. I'll wake
them all up when I get home to Kryston.'
She laid the rabbit gently into a padded
box and then popped a startled robin into
the cupboard.

A minute later the robin was free again
and Mandy was holding a limp copy of it
in her hands. She stared at the bird,
and the truth hit her all at once.

'It's a copying machine!' she blurted out.
'You're copying creatures and taking them
away with you! You're nothing but a
copycat, that's what you are!'

Amber looked at Mandy's indignant
face. 'I'll tell you a story,' she said, sitting
down on the log. And Mandy found
herself listening to the strangest tale she
had ever heard.

Amber came from a planet called Kryston, far away beyond the stars. There had been a war on Kryston, a terrible war between two great countries. When the war was finally over the air of the planet had been poisoned, and almost all its living creatures were dead.

'A few people and animals managed to stay alive in special shelters,' said Amber. 'Not very many, though.' She stared at the ground for a moment, then suddenly grinned.

'But here's the good bit, Mandy,'
she said. 'Kryston is recovering at last.
The air is pure again, grass is beginning
to grow . . .'

Mandy pushed the girl away furiously.
'And you're coming here pinching our
animals,' she shouted. 'That's stealing!'

Amber shook her head. 'I haven't taken one animal or bird,' she said. 'Only copies. Other people from my planet have gone to different countries on Earth, so that a complete collection can be made.'

She giggled suddenly. 'My dad's gone to Africa. To catch an elephant. That should be fun!'

'What about the camera?' demanded Mandy. 'How did you get into my school?'

'It was easy to forge false papers. It's all part of the plan,' said Amber eagerly. 'We're copying books and maps and stuff, so that we can learn about Earth people. We hope that one day our two planets can be friends.'

It all made sense. Mandy couldn't blame the Kryston people for what they were doing. And if the two planets really became friends, think of the things Earth people could learn from these creatures. Space travel, for a start . . .

She looked into the anxious golden
eyes. 'All right, Amber. I'll help,' she said.

There was a pause.

'There's something I haven't told you yet,
Mandy,' said Amber. 'What we need most
of all is people. I want to make copies of
young people like you, to work with us
and teach us about Earth.'

Mandy didn't wait to hear any more.
She fled from the clearing and ran home
so fast her feet hardly touched the ground.

4 Off to the Stars

Mandy paced around the living-room, biting her nails. *Battlestar Galactica* was on the telly, and as she gazed at the spaceships a lump came into her throat. Ever since she had left Amber Sunbeam alone in the woods she had felt sorry. Surely she could have let the cat-girl make a copy of her to take to Kryston. She would have been doing something really great for once. Something that would benefit all mankind.

'What on earth's the matter with you, Mandy?' said her mum crossly. 'You're making me dizzy.' She popped a chocolate into her mouth and fixed her eyes back on the screen.

Mandy's dad reached out for another can of beer. 'Got ants in her pants, has she?' he said. 'Here, Mandy, get yourself some chips. Give us a bit of peace for a change.'

Mandy caught the fifty-pence coin he threw at her and ran down the road.
It was a lovely evening, and the sky was pale pink on the horizon. There could be a copy of herself flying up there in a spaceship, to a planet beyond the stars, Mandy thought. If only she were brave enough.

She was so busy dreaming that she walked straight into somebody coming out of the chip-shop.

'Flippin' heck, Mandy! You almost knocked my chips into the road!'

It was Louise, clutching a large bag of chips to her chest. Mandy felt hungry.

'Wait till I get my chips, Lou,' she said. 'I've got something to tell you.'

As they strolled along together, Mandy told Louise about her afternoon's adventures.

Louise stopped with a chip halfway to her mouth.

'She wants to make a copy of you?' she squealed. 'And take it in the flying saucer? You wouldn't let her put you in that cupboard! You'd be scared to death!'

'Scared? Me?' laughed Mandy. 'I'm not scared. I've made up my mind to do it. Why don't you come, Lou? Think what fun two girls just like us could have with a new planet to explore.'

Louise made a gargling noise and
dashed away. Mandy took a deep breath,
flung her chips into the rubbish bin,
and ran towards Foxes Wood.

It was almost dark among the trees, but Mandy soon reached the clearing where the spaceship lay. Lights gleamed from its many windows, and streamed from the open doorway where Amber worked steadily on, packing her crates with woodland creatures. She turned when she heard Mandy's footsteps.

'You've come!' was all she said but Mandy knew how pleased she was by the quick flicking of her tail, and the sudden soft purr in her throat.

'Let's get on with it,' said Mandy, before
she changed her mind. She scrambled
into the cupboard and Amber shut the
door. There was a buzz and a flash of
green light. Mandy felt a sort of quiver
spread from her head to her toes. Then it
was all over.

Amber opened the door.

'Are you all right?' she said. 'Do you want to see the other you?'

Mandy nodded, unable to speak.

It was like having a twin sister, Mandy thought in wonder, staring at the sleeping figure who was her and yet not her. Numbly she helped Amber to lift the limp body into a box and carry it into the ship.

'Thanks, Mandy,' breathed Amber. 'You came just in time. We must say goodbye now. I'm almost ready to leave.'

Afterwards, Mandy could never remember exactly what happened next. She felt the cat-creature grabbing her in a goodbye hug, and then she was on the edge of the clearing with a roaring sound filling her ears.

The spaceship shuddered and slowly left the ground. It rose straight into the air until it was above the trees, then it suddenly streaked off into the evening sky towards the setting sun.

All was silent in Foxes Wood. Mandy stood for a long time gazing into the sky. Up there above the clouds was a girl who was part of her own self. She wondered what kind of life she would have, among strangers on a strange planet. And she couldn't help wondering if she would ever see her again.